ON LINE

03-6-04

JFICTION
Patte
Patterson, Nancy Ruth.

A simple gift /

BY NANCY RUTH PATTERSON

The Christmas Cup
Pictures by Leslie W. Bowman

The Shiniest Rock of All
Pictures by Karen A. Jerome

A Simple Gift

A SIMPLE GIFT

A SIMPLE GIFT

Nancy Ruth Patterson

Farrar, Straus and Giroux
New York

Thanks to Wesley Adams, Jonathan Diamond,
Pam Edmonds, Margaret Ferguson, Jere Lee
Hodgin, Katie McCabe, Mill Mountain Theatre,
Janet Renard, Molly Templeton, Christine Tomasino,
Jennifer Unter, and Tom Yezerski for their not-so-simple
gifts to this book
—N.R.P.

Library of Congress Cataloging-in-Publication Data
Patterson, Nancy Ruth.
    A simple gift / Nancy Ruth Patterson.— 1st ed.
        p.   cm.
    Summary: A small-town community theater production based on one
of her mother's books brings Carrie a glimpse of her mother's past and a
new understanding of giving to others.
    ISBN 0-374-36924-0
    [1. Theater—Fiction.   2. Authorship—Fiction.   3. Conduct of life—
Fiction.]   I. Title.

PZ7.P2769 Si 2003
[Fic]—dc21

                                                                        2002067156

For my family, friends, and former students, each of whom helped me carve initials into this mantel

And, especially, for my brother

I do remember

A SIMPLE GIFT

JUST THE RIGHT WORDS

"Mom, you'll *never* guess what!"

Carrie slammed the front door of their tenth-floor New York apartment so hard that her mother ran out of her office and rushed toward the living room, almost knocking over a drooping plant on the way.

"I got a part in my class play!" Carrie announced before her mother could possibly guess what. "And not just *any* part!" Carrie gasped, trying to catch her breath. "It's a *singing* part. And *guess* what I get to be?"

"May I have three guesses?" Mrs. O'Connor asked.

Carrie nodded. "And the first two don't even count."

"Little Red Riding Hood?"

"Guess again."

"Sleeping Beauty?"

"Nope. Better than that!"

"You're Peter Pan? That's who I wanted to be when I was your age . . . even if Peter Pan was a boy."

"You're not even close, Mom. Think really big!"

"Give me a hint."

"Okay." Carrie closed her eyes, concentrating hard. "What comes in threes?"

"Blind mice!" exclaimed Mrs. O'Connor.

"Mo-om!" Carrie could make the word last two syllables—or three, if she was really exasperated.

"Little pigs? You've been cast as a singing little pig?"

"Mo-oo-om!" The word lasted three syllables this time. "For your information, you are talking to a *molar*."

"A molar? As in teeth?"

As smart as she was, her mom sure could be clueless sometimes, Carrie thought.

"Yes, as in teeth."

"But most people have *twelve* molars, Carrie, not *three*! I'd have never guessed that in a million years."

"Yeah, but there are *three* up and *three* down on

each side." Carrie laughed, proud of her extra-hard hint. "Anyway, we're writing a play for National Children's Dental Health Month. Mrs. Gregory already thought of a name for it."

"Which is?"

"*The Tooth, the Whole Tooth, and Nothing but the Tooth,*" Carrie said cautiously. "We really didn't like the title all that much, Mom, but we didn't want to hurt our teacher's feelings, she was so proud of it."

"I kind of like the title," Mom said. "It's so"—she struggled for the right word—"so *unforgettable.*"

"And I, Ann McCarrity O'Connor, better known as Carrie, am a *molar*. It's one of the most important roles. I'm the only tooth that sings."

"And what exactly do you sing?" asked Mrs. O'Connor.

"I've got to make up the song myself," she said. "I think the teacher picked me to write it because . . . because you're a real writer and she figured you could help."

"Well, let's see if I can."

Mrs. O'Connor walked to the office, where she did her writing, and motioned for Carrie to follow. Inside, she nodded for Carrie to sit down at the desk. Carrie dropped her book bag to the floor and settled herself in her mother's writing chair, which she considered the best seat in the house.

"So where do I begin?" Carrie asked.

"I always think of what I want to say first. Then I figure out exactly how to say it. Just get something down on paper, Carrie. You can always change it later." She cleared away pages filled with scribbling and put a fresh pad of paper in front of Carrie. Then she sat down in a chair on the other side of the desk.

Carrie looked around the office. The dozen Michael Madigan books her mother had written were lined up neatly on the bookshelf along the wall. On the desk lay a stack of letters from children who had read those books. Mrs. O'Connor always answered every letter, though sometimes she didn't get it done too quickly. Carrie saw the well-worn dictionary, creased open to the W's. Then she saw that picture, the one that had gotten her in such trouble a few weeks before—the faded photo of a boy holding a fish on a cane pole with one hand and clutching the fingers of a pigtailed girl with the other. It had been on her mother's desk for as long as Carrie could remember . . . until the night when Carrie had accidentally knocked it off and cracked the frame. Usually when Carrie did something wrong, her mother's disappointment just bubbled up. But that night it had boiled over big-time. Carrie didn't really understand why her mother was so upset over a little thing like that picture frame. She had broken lots of other things before . . . a crystal lamp, a porcelain rabbit, even her big toe. Her mother hadn't ever made such a big deal out of anything. True, Carrie had suggested that a breeze had blown the frame off the desk, until her mother pointed out that the windows were closed. But when Carrie finally confessed, you'd have thought the frame was made of pure gold instead of Popsicle sticks.

"So what do you want to say about teeth?" Mom's question from across the desk prodded Carrie's thoughts away from the picture and back to the play.

"Most grown-ups have thirty-two of them. Brush after every meal. In circles. Not too hard. Not too soft. Remember to floss. That's very important, too."

"Well, there's your raw material. Now think of a tune you like. Something everybody knows. Like 'Row, Row, Row Your Boat.' Everybody knows that one, Carrie."

"Brush, brush, brush your teeth," Carrie began timidly, looking at her mother for approval. Mrs. O'Connor nodded for her to go on.

Carrie couldn't think of a second line. "Maybe I've got writer's block," she said. Her mother always said that when she got stuck.

"Morning, noon, and night . . ." Mrs. O'Connor suggested. She had to add the third line, too. "If you treat your teeth like friends . . ."

She paused, wanting Carrie to finish the song. "Now what rhymes with night, Carrie?" she asked.

"Fight. Sight. Tight. Right." Carrie was good at rhyming. "That's it, Mom. Right!" She sang the last line herself. "Then they will treat you right."

"Oh no!" Mrs. O'Connor groaned playfully. "Not another writer in the family!"

"Now I want to write a song all by myself," said Carrie. Ever since she could talk, "by myself" had been one of Carrie's favorite things to say.

"You just stay right at my desk while I get supper ready," said Mrs. O'Connor. "Your father has to work late at the hospital tonight."

"D.D. always has to work late at the hospital," said Carrie, shrugging her bony shoulders. She called her father D.D. instead of Dad or Daddy. When she was little, Carrie had first called him D.D. on the very day he graduated from medical school. Her father told people D.D. stood for Doctor Dad. Carrie knew it was really just baby talk, like the way she had said "boon" for balloon or "baw" for ball. But she loved it whenever he told someone that story.

Her mother ignored Carrie's comment about the hospital. "So what would you like to eat?"

"Pasketti!" Carrie laughed. She never grew tired of her mother's spaghetti.

"Pasketti," agreed Mrs. O'Connor. "I'll just get the sauce started and be right back to see what you've come up with."

Carrie used her mother's fancy black fountain pen to jot ideas onto the yellow pad of paper—just like her mother did. Then she crossed out some words—just like her mother did. Then she balled up the piece of paper and tossed it across the room at a wastebasket. Her mother always did that, too. "Two points for me," she said to herself when the shot went in.

By the time the smell of sautéing onions and garlic was drifting through the apartment, Carrie had written the perfect lyrics for her song. She typed them up neatly on her mother's computer, which was on one side of the desk. Her mother could type without looking at the keys. Carrie typed very slowly, using one finger.

When her mother returned, Carrie handed her the sheet of paper. "You sing it to the tune of 'Twinkle, Twinkle, Little Star,' " she explained.

Mrs. O'Connor first read Carrie's words aloud slowly:

> *Twinkle, twinkle, little tooth.*
> *We all need you, that's the truth.*

You must be brushed and flossed just right,
Morning, afternoon, and night.

Then Mom began to sing the words. Carrie joined in and they sang the song over and over, faster and faster, until they both dissolved into giggles.

Her mother hugged Carrie before she could squirm away.

"I just love it when my words come out right," Carrie said proudly, folding the paper precisely into a little square and sticking it into a folder inside her book bag.

2

A Star Is Born

"So did you *really* think I was good?" Carrie asked her father as they walked the five blocks from the Holcomb School to their apartment after the class play. Her mother held one of Carrie's hands while they waited for a crosswalk light to change from red; her father held the other. It was late, past Carrie's bedtime, but the streets were still filled with the sound of honking taxis and the diesel smell of buses that whooshed by now and then. Carrie looked at the three-foot-tall tooth costume D.D. held in his other hand. It really did resemble a molar, with its broad cratered top and its creamy color. Carrie had made it from papier-mâché in art class all by herself.

"You were absolutely terrific," D.D. said. "My daughter was absolutely terrific!" he shouted to no one in particular.

The night was warm for February, and Carrie could almost feel spring around the corner.

"You'd get my vote for molar of the year," her mother added. "Especially that 'toe heel, toe heel, shuffle' dance part. That really was a showstopper, Carrie."

Carrie hadn't been sure about that part. She was glad her mother liked it.

A man passing by looked at Carrie's costume and then smiled at her. "I hope the tooth fairy leaves you a lot of money for that one," he teased.

Carrie laughed and imagined how much a tooth this size might be worth. A hundred dollars? The most she had ever gotten for a baby tooth was a dollar, though her best friend, Holland, always got two when she put hers under the pillow. She wished Holland hadn't moved away.

Every few steps Carrie would sing another line from her song, pulling on her parents' hands to get them to walk in time to the music.

"We must look strange, walking like this," D.D. said with a laugh.

"Nobody will notice if we act strange. It's New York City." Carrie's mother wasn't complaining. She always said things like that about New York, and Carrie knew she wouldn't really want to live anywhere else.

"Do you wish you had grown up here?" Carrie asked her father.

"I liked growing up in Missouri. I just wish we could go back there more often to visit your grandma and grandpa."

"Mom, you were born in North Carolina, right?"

"In Brownsville, North Carolina, honey. A little town not too far from Asheville. We moved from there when I was about your age, and I haven't been back since. They must still remember me, though."

"What makes you say that, Mom?"

"Because they want to make one of my books into a children's play for their Fourth of July homecoming. The town will be a hundred and fifty years old this year, Carrie, and they want to produce a play as part of the big celebration. A director called me about producing it last week."

"You're going to let them, aren't you, Mom?"

"Probably. I've never let anyone make one of my books into a play before, but I knew this director a long time ago. He has a wonderful reputation on Broadway, and I'd trust him to do it right."

"Which book?"

"Michael Madigan's Curtain Call."

"It's my favorite! Are you going to Brownsville to see it?"

"I'd like to, but I don't know. I've got a deadline for my new book the first of August, Carrie, and you know how crazy it gets around deadline time."

Carrie's mind began whirring with excitement, and after a couple of blocks she couldn't contain herself. "Will there be kids my age in the play?" she asked.

"I suppose so. There are ten-year-old kids in my books."

"Do you think I could be in it?"

"Oh, honey, I don't think so. North Carolina's so far away. Besides, I wouldn't want people to think you got a part just because you're the author's daughter."

"What if I tried out for the play and nobody even knew who I was and I got a role all by myself? I could change my name to something catchy, like Carrie Berry or Carrie Perry." Carrie saw her mother smile. "You write under a different name; why can't I use a different one, too?"

"Kate McCarrity isn't a pen name," her mother explained. "It's the name I was born with. I had written several books before I married your father, and I just kept on writing under the name readers knew me by."

"Please, Mom," Carrie begged. "I want to try out for that play more than I've ever wanted anything."

"It takes a long time to rehearse for a play, Carrie. A couple of weeks at least. We couldn't leave D.D. that long."

"D.D.'s always working at the hospital anyway." When she saw her father wince, Carrie was sorry she had said it. "We could call him every night, and he could fly down on the Fourth of July to see me in the play," she said, her voice full of enthusiasm. "It would be so much fun, and I just know I could get a part. You said I was absolutely terrific tonight, didn't you?"

"We'll think about it," her parents both said at the same time. When her father said those words, it almost always meant no. When her mother said them, it meant maybe.

"I've decided I want to be an actress," Carrie said as they turned into their apartment building. "Besides, Michael Madigan's almost like a brother to me. He'd want me to try out." When her parents didn't respond, Carrie tried hard to pout, but she couldn't keep back a smile when D.D. introduced her to their doorman as Madame Molar.

A half hour later, before she drifted off to sleep, Carrie yelled from her bedroom, "If *I* were the mother, I'd let *you* try out!"

3

A Big Deal

"Why didn't you tell me it was such a big deal?" was the first thing Carrie said when she saw the poster in the lobby of the old hotel where she and her mother were staying on the Brownsville square. It was summer vacation, four months after she first heard about the play.

"Because you didn't ask me," Mrs. O'Connor said.

Carrie ran her fingers over the words on the poster and read them aloud slowly:

Auditions for
Brownsville's 150th Anniversary Homecoming Play
Michael Madigan's Curtain Call
Performances: July 3–10

Based on the best-selling children's book
by Brownsville's *OWN* Award-Winning Writer
Kate McCarrity

Directed by Brownsville's *OWN* Award-Winning
Director L. Bennett Sanders

At the Apple Barn Theater

Then in smaller type the poster said:

Roles for
One adult female (any age)
Two boys, age 8–11
Three girls, age 8–11
And one very smart dog (any age)

At the Apple Barn Theater
Saturday, June 15, at noon

Bring bio and recent photo.
All those auditioning (except the dogs) should
memorize a short poem or monologue.

Carrie's mother grabbed the handles of their two
big suitcases and began to roll them from the lobby
down the hall to their room. Carrie followed, lug-
ging a smaller suitcase that didn't have wheels. The

Brownsville Hotel didn't look anything like the hotels Carrie was accustomed to seeing in New York. The lobby was about the size of her bedroom at home, and the old wooden floors creaked. Their room at the end of the hall had white ruffled curtains, and an old quilt with a pattern shaped like a star was draped across the end of each twin bed. The sink in their bathroom sat on a pedestal, and the tub stood on four claws. Her mother switched on a ceiling fan and pushed open two windows. "I'd almost forgotten how good mountain air smelled," she said as she scraped her fingers lightly across the rusted window screen.

Carrie almost wished her father hadn't let her come here. He had said she would make a good lawyer, the way she had argued with him so much about coming. First, she had asked him, "What if Shirley Temple's mother hadn't let her try out for her first show?" Carrie knew that D.D. liked old Shirley Temple movies even more than she did, but he hadn't even answered. Then she told him the pure mountain air would be good for her asthma. She figured since he was a doctor, the argument would really get to him. "I almost suffocated last summer in New York, it was so hot," she had said, clutching her throat and making choking sounds for effect. "You're getting to be a better actress all the time," D.D. had said. Then she had reminded him how grouchy Mom got when she had another book to finish. "Your deadlines almost kill *me*," she had said, imitating her father's deep voice.

Carrie never could figure out why it took her mother so long to write a book. D.D. joked that he could finish six surgeries in the time it took her mother to finish six sentences. "What do you *do* all day?" he had asked her more than once.

When Carrie was a toddler, her parents had hired a nanny to come and look after her in the apartment during the day so her mother could work at home. Carrie came to visit her mother in the office almost every hour, begging to sit beside her as she leaned over the computer. Sometimes her mother would lift Carrie on her lap and let her tiny fingers slap out nonsense words on the keyboard. Most of the time, though, Carrie had to be so quiet in her mother's office that she called it the hush room. "*Shushhhhh*," her mother would say gently when she toddled in, asking her to read *Goodnight Moon* aloud for the tenth time that day. "*Shushhhhh*, Mommy has a deadline; she has to finish her book."

Carrie had no idea why anyone would want to be a writer. It was fun to write for a little while, when the words came out right, like when she wrote her molar song. But to do it all the time must be the loneliest job in the whole world, she thought, just sitting in a room by yourself all day, typing away, with nobody to keep you company except the imaginary people you were pecking out on the keyboard. She wondered if her mother would ever run out of ideas for her books. If she did, then maybe she would get a real job, like Mary Ellen's mother, who worked at a television station, or Maggie's, who sold clothes at a store on Fifth Avenue.

In truth, Carrie knew it wasn't her pleading but rather her mother's desire that had gotten her to North Carolina. She knew her mother had wanted to come back to Brownsville, though from what she had seen from the window of the Ford rental car on the two-hour drive from the airport in Asheville, Carrie couldn't imagine why. She missed the busyness of New York already. Everything here seemed so old. Everything seemed so small. Everything seemed so quiet.

"If nobody lives in Brownsville, then who will come to see the play?" Carrie asked. She was remembering a sign on the way into town: BROWNS-VILLE, NORTH CAROLINA—POPULATION 3,200.

"Lots of people come here for summer vacations," her mother explained. The square was almost deserted. Carrie guessed their vacations hadn't started yet.

"All right, Madame Molar"—her mother and father called her that all the time now—"we'll have to unpack later. Can't be late for auditions. They're very strict about this kind of thing in the theater.

Let's hear your poem one more time before you go. Say it loud, Carrie, and put more expression into it this time."

Carrie made her words come out as clearly as she could: "I have a little shadow that goes in and out with me . . . And what can be the use of him is more than I can see."

Carrie shrugged her shoulders when she got to that part. "He is very, very like me from the heels up to the head . . ."

Carrie pointed first to her feet and then touched her head with her index finger. "And I see him jump before me, when I jump into my bed."

She gave a little hop, pretending to look up at her shadow on the wall. She started again, this time saying all the verses.

"Oh!" exclaimed Carrie suddenly. "I forgot to say that my poem was by Robert Louis Stevenson." Then she gave a little curtsy.

Mom clapped. "Don't forget your picture," she reminded Carrie, pulling it from a suitcase. It was a large print of Carrie's school picture from third grade and looked pretty good, if you didn't count the front teeth that weren't there. Her teeth weren't missing anymore, but since the picture from the fourth-grade year had hair flyaways, she had picked last year's photo instead.

———

"I've been saving the article from the newspaper for you, Mrs. O'Connor. It came out right after you made your reservation here," said the man at the desk. He handed them the newspaper. "You made the front page!" He seemed friendlier than he had when they checked in earlier, Carrie thought. "It took me a few minutes to realize who you were after you came in," he said. "Nice to have you in town."

Carrie's mother threw open the newspaper and began to read aloud.

BACK HOME AGAIN!

BROADWAY DIRECTOR AND BEST-SELLING CHILDREN'S AUTHOR RETURN TO BROWNSVILLE FOR HOMECOMING PLAY

By Willeyne McCune
Special Correspondent to *Mountain Views*

L. Bennett Sanders left Brownsville for Broadway. Kate McCarrity left Brownsville for the best-seller list. This summer's 150th anniversary celebration brings them both back home for the world premiere of a play he will adapt from her beloved children's book *Michael Madigan's Curtain Call.*

"When Apple Barn Theater approached me about the project, I jumped at the chance," said the award-winning stage director. "I want to give back to the town that gave me my start and to visit with my family and old friends," Sanders said. "I'm also very honored that Kate McCarrity will allow me to take her treasured book from the page to the stage."

His parents, Mr. and Mrs. Broady Sanders, say they are proud of their son's success in the theater. "I knew right away he didn't take to farming," said his father. His mother says she wishes he didn't live so far away from them. "This is the first time he has come back to Brownsville in a long time. We went to see one of his plays last year in New York," she said, "but New York's too noisy for me. I couldn't sleep a wink with those horns honking all night."

Kate McCarrity O'Connor, who writes under her maiden name, Kate McCarrity, also currently lives in New York City. She went to school in Brownsville before moving with her parents after the fourth grade.

Mrs. Dorothy Meyer, her third-grade teacher, remembers her as an outstanding student. "She was the best writer in the class. I wish I had kept at least one of her papers," she said.

Mrs. Wallace Barrett sat beside her in the fourth grade. "I always knew Kate would be somebody important," she said.

McCarrity's twelve children's books have all found their way onto the best-seller list. *Michael Madigan's Curtain Call* won the coveted Mountaineer Award for being voted favorite novel of the year by elementary school students in North Carolina.

The play will be produced at the Apple Barn Theater July 3–10. Auditions for the roles of three boys, three girls, and one adult will be held there on June 15 at noon. The director says he's also looking for one smart dog to complete the cast.

4

CASTING CALL

Carrie and her mother walked almost a mile from their hotel to the Apple Barn Theater. Her mother had said the long walk would calm them both. Carrie didn't talk much on the way; she was trying to practice her poem over and over in her head, along with imaginary toe points and shoulder shrugs, so she wouldn't forget anything when it came time to audition. Lots of cars were in the parking lot when they reached the theater. It didn't look like Carnegie Hall or Lincoln Center, but Carrie thought the building was pretty grand all the same, with its bright red paint and all sorts of banners and flags flapping in the breeze. This place had been an old apple barn at one time, her mother had told her, before it had been turned into one of the best summer-stock theaters in the South. Pictures of actors who had performed there were posted prominently in a large display case out front. At first Carrie wasn't exactly sure who they were, but she thought she recognized one or two from old movies on TV.

Carrie dropped her mother's hand as they walked up to the big porch of the theater, where at least fifty children and two dozen dogs stood in line. Carrie tried to count them. The children all had pictures in their hands.

"I'm going to recite the preamble to the Constitution for my tryout," Carrie heard a tall boy say when he handed his picture to the cheerful-looking woman who smiled at him from behind the registration table. The boy was wearing blue pants, a white shirt, and a red bandanna, and he carried a tall hat with red, white, and blue stripes on it.

"I'm going to say 'The Homework Machine' by Shel Silverstein," said a tiny girl with a Band-Aid on her index finger.

"That's what *I'm* going to use," said a girl in a denim jumper standing behind her in line. "My mother said it would be so *original*."

"That's just fine," said the woman at the registration table. "The director loves Shel Silverstein's work. Why, he told me himself that he never gets tired of hearing that poem."

Carrie looked at twins dressed in identical white sailor suits with big navy bows.

"Wouldn't it be just awful if one of them got a part and the other one didn't?" Carrie whispered to her mother.

"I guess that's one good thing about being an only child," her mother whispered back.

Another girl who waited in line was carrying a toilet plunger. Carrie wondered why. A boy squirmed as his mother spit on her finger and tried to smooth down his cowlick.

"Everybody else seems to know somebody," said Carrie as she inched closer to the registration table. Suddenly, she felt very alone. She wished D.D. were here, calling her Madame Molar and telling her she was absolutely terrific.

"You've got me . . . and you've got your little shadow," her mother said, trying to coax the corners of Carrie's mouth into a smile.

A mother standing in front of Carrie was spelling her daughter's name to be sure the woman at the table wrote it down right. "Barrett. B-A-double-R-E-double-T. Her first name's Liza. L-I-Z-A." Liza wore a pretty dress like the ones in store windows along Fifth Avenue in New York, and Carrie thought she looked more sophisticated than some of her friends at Holcomb. "Liza's been taking dancing lessons for years," the mother said. "She's been in lots of recitals. You will tell the director that, won't you? And she's in lots of ads for the newspaper her father owns. People just love those ads. You'll tell the director about that, too, won't you?"

The woman at the table smiled and handed Liza a number. "Pin this number on your collar," she said. "Ben uses numbers, not names, just to be fair. And I don't have to tell Ben Sanders anything. He can spot talent for himself from a mile off." She smiled when she said it, adding Liza's photo to the growing pile on the table, weighed down with a brick to keep all the pictures from blowing away. Then she excused herself and went to organize the dogs. A rowdy collie and a boxer were running around the porch, chasing each other and barking. A small white poodle stood calmly by a boy who was slapping a leash gently against the side of a tree. The boy looked scruffier than the other kids. His mop of hair sprawled all over his head . . . all catywumpus, her mother would say. The dog, on the other hand, looked as manicured as the boy looked messy. The poodle seemed content; the boy, for all his scowling and scruffiness, seemed nervous.

"I can't believe *he's* going to try out," Liza whined loudly to her mother. "After what happened at school and everything!"

Carrie wondered what had happened at school, but she didn't dare ask.

"They should have named him Hurricane instead of Storm!" said Mrs. Barrett, shaking her head. "I wonder where he got that poodle?"

"He probably *stole* him," Liza said in a voice so loud everyone on the porch could hear. Storm looked first at Liza. Then he looked down at the little dog, pulling softly at his ear, rubbing him around the neck. Then he walked away from the theater, the dog close by his heels.

"Do you think his real name's Storm?" Carrie said to her mother. She'd never heard a name like that before.

Her mother shrugged. "His dog seems to like him well enough, whatever his real name is."

"You sure nobody will know I'm your daughter?" Carrie asked suddenly. Nobody had seemed to recognize her mother yet. Carrie supposed she'd been away from Brownsville so long people didn't even know who she was. "I want to get this role *all by myself*, Mom."

"I'm sure, Carrie. I haven't seen Ben Sanders for thirty years. And you just heard that he uses numbers, not names, for auditions anyway. You don't even have to be Carrie Berry . . . or was it Carrie Perry?" She smiled. "If you get a part, you'll get it *all by yourself*." She straightened the collar of the blue-and-white-striped blouse peeking out of Carrie's khaki jumper. "I'll wait for you over there, underneath that oak." She pointed to a tree about a hundred yards away. "I brought along a book to read in case you're gone awhile." Carrie knew her mother would bring along a book to read. She read everywhere she went. Waiting in line for the bus. Propped against a wall in the subway station. During intermission of the Knicks game at Madison Square Garden. "Talk about bookworms," D.D. had said when she did that.

"O'Connor. Carrie O'Connor." She said her name slowly when the woman at the table asked her who she was and gave her the number 48 to pin on her blouse. But she didn't try to spell it. Carrie was so scared that she wasn't sure she could remember how.

5

ALMOST AWESOME

It was still dark when Carrie pulled a sweatsuit over her pajamas and tiptoed to the phone booth in the lobby of the hotel. She put two quarters in the slot and carefully dialed the number they had given everyone after auditions were over. When the answering machine finally clicked on, she heard a scratchy pause. Then Ben Sanders's voice came on the tape. "These people have been selected for the cast of *Curtain Call* and should report for rehearsals at noon today. The dog has not yet been chosen." Carrie took a deep breath. "Liza Barrett. Margaret Blake." Another deep breath. "Jeremy Jones." Ben was saying names in alphabetical order, she realized. Her heart was racing. "Carrie O'Connor." *Carrie*

O'Connor! Carrie didn't even listen for the other names. She hung up the receiver and raced back down the hall to their room, the floor creaking behind her.

"Mom!" Carrie stage-whispered as loud as she dared when she flew in the doorway. "I got a part. I'm in the cast. I've got to be at the Apple Barn for rehearsals at noon today."

"What time is it, Carrie?" asked Mrs. O'Connor, rubbing her eyes and pulling the quilt to her chin.

"Five o'clock. Can I call D.D.?"

"At five o'clock in the morning?"

"Just this once? Please . . ."

After a big yawn, Mrs. O'Connor got out of bed and hugged Carrie to her.

"Congratulations, honey. I'm proud of you," Mrs. O'Connor said as she pulled the quilt around her like a robe and followed Carrie to the phone booth in the lobby. They both crammed onto the tiny seat and waited for Dr. O'Connor to answer their collect call. "Your father's not a morning person," said her mother. "I always told him he should have been a skin doctor so he wouldn't get so many emergency calls in the middle of the night."

"Hullo," D.D. finally answered after the tenth ring. Carrie could tell that he wasn't really awake yet.

"I got a part," Carrie said. She felt like shouting the good news, but was afraid of waking up the other guests. Like the hotel itself, most of the people staying there seemed really old, and her mother had already warned her that the guests had come here for peace and quiet. Carrie tried to whisper enthusiastically instead. "And I got it all by myself!"

"That's great, honey," her father said. "What time is it?"

Mrs. O'Connor gently took the phone away from Carrie. "You better make plane reservations for opening night," she said to her husband. "They might be hard to get for the Fourth of July weekend."

Carrie heard her mother mumble "Uh-huh" a few times. Then she said, "Say goodbye to Carrie," and handed the phone back.

"If you're happy, then I'm happy, too," said D.D., a little more awake now. "I'll see you in a couple of weeks, Madame Molar."

Carrie could see a car driving around the square, its lights flashing shadows into the lobby while they talked. The lobby didn't seem so dark anymore.

Carrie sat in a circle on the Apple Barn stage, looking at the man in the middle. "As you know, my name's L. Bennett Sanders," he said, "but you may call me Ben. I'll be directing this play. I want to know who you are. So come up to center stage one by one." He pointed to a spot with a big X taped on it. "I want you to clap your hands and jump out a little, like this." He showed them what to do. "And shout really loud—so loud they can hear you in Asheville—'Hi. My name's so-and-so and I'm *awesome!*' And say it so I'll believe you really *are* awesome." Ben was a handsome man with graying hair and kind eyes. "Who wants to go first?"

"Hi." A loud clap. "My name's Liza, and I'm *awesome*." She curtsied.

"Hi." Another loud clap. "I'm J.J., and I'm *awesome*, too." The boy tipped his Yankees cap and took a little bow.

"Hi." The next boy jumped out, but he forgot to clap. "I'm Matt. I'm *unbelievably* awesome." He looked embarrassed after he said it.

Then it was Carrie's turn. She walked to center stage and looked out into the almost empty rows of seats. "Hi," she said. But she knew she hadn't said it loudly enough. "Could I start over?" she asked. "I think I can do it better this time."

Ben nodded.

Carrie cleared her throat. "Hi!" This time the word came out louder. She hopped forward. "I'm

Carrie, and I'm awesome!" She smiled a nervous smile and walked off as quickly as she could.

Yonah, a girl two years younger than Carrie, was awesome, too.

An older woman, about the same age as Carrie's teacher in New York, said her name was Margaret. When she said she was awesome, you really believed it! Carrie wished she could make her words come out like that.

"This is Kelly Clemens," Ben said, pointing to the woman sitting beside him. "She's the stage manager, and she is incredibly awesome!" The way Ben said it, you knew she really was. "Who knows what a stage manager does?" No one answered. "A stage manager is in charge of everyone and everything that happens in a play—she's my assistant. She even helped me write the script. It's my job to get you ready for opening night, but after that, Kelly takes over. She's the boss. So if you've got any questions, Kelly's got the answers."

Kelly began handing out thick scripts, each one bound like a spiral notebook.

"Let me tell you a little about the play we're doing," Ben said, looking around the circle of actors. "Have any of you read *Michael Madigan's Curtain Call*?" Carrie waited for someone else to speak first.

"We read it in the third grade," said Liza. "The woman who wrote it went to school in Brownsville when she was little. I forgot what her name is, but our teacher told us all about her. My mother said her family was so poor she didn't even have money for *pencils and paper*."

Carrie felt herself frowning. She wanted to stick up for her mother, but she didn't know what she should say.

"What do you remember about the book?" asked Ben, ignoring Liza's comment about the author.

"It's about this popular boy who gets to be the star in the school play. Only he pretends that he has a sore throat so a kid named Louis the Loser can take his place at the last minute."

"What made him do that?" asked Ben.

"I forget," said Liza, "but I remember thinking it was a dumb thing to do."

"It wasn't dumb," said Carrie loudly. "Michael Madigan knew how much Louis wanted the part, and he felt sorry for him because Louis was so unpopular. So Michael figured out a way that Louis could be the star so people wouldn't think he was a loser anymore."

"Maybe Michael said he had a sore throat because he was really scared to be onstage in front of all those people," said Yonah. She hadn't actually read the book, she admitted, but she thought that could be the reason anyway.

Carrie could feel her temper rising. "Michael wasn't scared of anything!" she retorted.

"How do you think Michael felt when he saw everyone clapping for Louis when the play ended?" Ben asked.

"He probably felt stupid because everybody could have been clapping for him," Matt guessed.

"He didn't feel stupid!" shouted Carrie.

"It's wrong to tell a lie," said J.J. His father was a preacher, and he knew about such things. "Michael Madigan told a lie about having a sore throat."

"He didn't lie," Carrie responded. "He didn't even say one word. He just pointed to his throat and acted like he was sick. Michael was such a good actor, everyone believed him. And Michael Madigan felt good when Louis got the applause because he knew"—Carrie struggled to find the right words— "he knew he had done something . . . noble."

"And what was that?" asked Ben.

"He gave someone else something he really wanted himself."

"How come you know so much about Michael Madigan anyway?" asked Liza. Carrie felt her face flush.

"Because my mother wrote the book," she heard

herself say. "And your teacher got it all wrong. My mother wasn't that poor, and you can tell her that I, Ann McCarrity O'Connor, said so." Carrie felt like running off the stage and all the way back to New York.

"Carrie O'Connor. Kate McCarrity O'Connor's daughter. I had no idea who you were when you tried out." Ben chuckled, shaking his head. "I really didn't."

"My mother and I wanted it that way," Carrie said slowly, looking down into her lap. "I wanted to get a role all by myself."

"Do you know her mother?" asked Yonah.

"Not very well," said Ben, "but I knew her mother's brother a long time ago."

Carrie knew everyone was staring at her. Especially Liza. She could feel her stare from across the stage.

"We've got work to do," said Ben, changing the subject. "They call what we're doing a *play*, but you'll probably think it's the hardest *work* you've ever done." He looked around to be sure everyone was listening. "Kelly has handed out the script. We've just got two and a half weeks until opening night. We'll rehearse almost all day, and some of you will have to run through your scenes at night, too. We don't have a minute to waste, so let's get started. Kelly will ask you to read different scenes in the play. Just relax and do your best. We're still not certain who we want to cast in what role, so we need to hear you all read different parts in the play before we decide."

"Which role is biggest?" asked Liza.

"There's an old saying around the theater that there's no such thing as a small *role*, just small *actors*." He winked when he said it.

"Then which character has the most lines?"

"I suppose that would be Michael Madigan."

"So whoever gets to be Michael Madigan gets to be the *star*!" J.J. blurted out.

"But Michael Madigan's a *boy*!" said Liza. "How come a *girl* can't be the star?"

Ben didn't answer. He looked first at one person, then another. His stare lingered a long time on Liza. The theater sounded so quiet you could hear Ben breathing; Carrie could tell that Ben hadn't liked the question.

"All the *stars* can leave right now," Ben said finally. No one moved. "Then everyone who's not a star can turn to Act 2, Scene 3. Yonah, you read Katherine's part, and J.J., you be Michael Madigan. Then we'll switch off until everyone has read."

Ben and Kelly took notes on a yellow tablet while each person read aloud. Carrie thought J.J. and Liza read the best. She wondered what Ben thought.

"That's enough for now," Ben said. "I'll tell you tomorrow morning who will be playing what role. And remember . . . there are no small roles, only . . ." He paused and waited for everyone to help him finish the sentence.

"Small actors!" they shouted together.

Ben clapped. Then he said the word better than Carrie had ever heard it said before.

"Awesome!"

6

WAITING FOR THE STORM

It was hot outside. Carrie sat by herself on a step just inside the back exit of the dark theater, where it was cool, waiting for her mother to pick her up after the first rehearsal. Sometimes when she was working on a book, her mother forgot about the time. But since Carrie was too tired to walk back to the hotel by herself, she just waited. The door was open but there was no breeze. Behind her, in the funnel of the stage light, she could see Ben unzip his canvas briefcase and stuff an inch-thick stack of papers inside. "I guess I've got my night's reading cut out for me," she heard him say.

"You've got a good cast," said Kelly, sitting down

beside Ben. "Not exactly *awesome* yet, but they've got over *two whole weeks* to get that way." She smiled at Ben, then picked up her pen. "So who's Michael Madigan?" Carrie wondered if she should say something to let them know she was still around, or maybe just creep outside quietly to keep from hearing their secrets. But her curiosity won out, and she slouched over to make herself even more invisible in the darkness.

"J.J. read the best, but he's not quite right for the part. Can't put my finger on it exactly, but I just don't picture Michael Madigan looking like that. Maybe J.J.'s a little *too* handsome for the role."

"I could ugly him up," teased Kelly. "Break his nose in a couple of places . . . anything for the play, you know." Ben laughed as Kelly smacked at the air with her fists.

"What we need is—" Ben stopped in midsentence. First he heard the bark. Then he saw the boy.

"Is someone who looks exactly like him," Ben and Kelly said at the same time as Storm Sellers walked from the back of the theater into the spill of the spotlight.

"I know the tryouts were yesterday, but I came by to see if my dog Newby could still get a role in that play you're putting on," said the boy, scooping his poodle up under his arm without even looking down.

"What's your name?"

"Storm. Storm Sellers."

Kelly and Ben looked surprised at the sound of his name.

"That your real name?"

"You making fun of it, mister?" Storm's voice ricocheted off the rafters.

"It's just that I've never known anyone named Storm before," Ben said. "How did you get that name?"

"Mom says I was born during a real bad rain and all the lights went out in the hospital for a couple of seconds. And the doctor, he handed me to my mother and said, 'Mrs. Sellers, we've had ourselves quite a storm.'" He paused, shielding his eyes from the spotlight. "So my mom, she named me after what the doctor said." He laughed. "Said Storm and Sellers went together real good . . . like peanut butter and jelly." Storm put Newby on the stage floor. "I like my name . . . fits me good."

"And Newby . . . how'd he get his name?"

"Didn't name him myself."

"Who did?"

"Lady I got him from, she named him, I guess."

"How'd he come to be yours?"

"Uncle Will took care of a cabin on Cattail Creek where this lady came to spend the summers . . . just her and this dog. She got sick one night and went to the hospital. Never came back. Uncle Will, he brought Newby home to live with us. Been there ever since."

Newby looked up at Storm and barked twice. Storm scratched around his collar. "Good boy," he said softly as Newby licked him on the cheek.

"Tell us about Newby," Ben said as Storm climbed the stairs to the stage, still shielding his eyes from the light. "I sure do like his haircut."

Storm softened his scowl. "Thanks, mister," he said. "There's this lady in town . . . she charges more to clip a dog than Betty charges for a haircut over at the Beauty Bazaar—not that I go there too often." He laughed a little. "Only she don't charge me nothing to cut Newby's hair because I mow her grass for free. We made a deal." Carrie watched as Storm tickled Newby's chin again. "Even Uncle Will says she gussies him up real good."

"How smart is he?" Ben asked.

"Smartest dog in the county," said Storm. Newby barked again, begging for another scratch. "A little prissified, maybe, but real smart. Smarter than most people I know."

"Smart enough to bark on cue?"

Storm looked confused. Then a smile crossed his face.

"Smart enough to bark on any letter you say . . . Q, R, S, or T . . . any of them."

Kelly laughed just a little before she saw that Storm was being dead serious.

"So he'll bark anytime you ask him to?"

"One bark means yes. Two barks mean no. He can lie down and sit and shake hands, too." Storm let Newby down onto the stage.

"When we looked at the dogs people brought to auditions yesterday, we were really looking for a bigger dog."

"Look, mister. The poster at the gas station, it said you were looking for a *smart* dog. Didn't say *big*. Didn't say *little*. Said *smart*. No dog around here smarter than Newby."

"What makes you think Newby wants to be in this play?"

" 'Cause then everybody'd know how smart he is, and he'd—he'd—" Storm stammered and looked down, first at his boots, next at the little dog nipping at the cuffs of his jeans. Then he finished his sentence. "He'd be real proud of himself."

"Ever think of being in a play yourself?"

"No way, mister. I hate that kind of stuff."

"Takes more courage to face an audience than it takes to face a mountain lion, some people say." Ben waited until his words sank in. "You wouldn't be scared of a little old audience, would you, Storm?"

"Not scared of nothing, mister."

"What do you think, Kelly? Do you think we could use a little dog in the play, a smart little dog?"

"I think a little dog might do."

"There might be a part for you, too, Storm."

"Uh-uh, mister. I'm no actor. Don't even like to read."

"I bet you've got a good memory. We could teach you to memorize your lines. That way, you wouldn't have to read them if you didn't want to."

"Uncle Will, he says I never forget anything. After I've seen an ad on TV once I can say all the lines before the actors even say them. I never miss a word. Uncle Will says he's never seen anything like it."

"I've got a good feeling about you, Storm. You've got a great voice. Loud and clear. And you look like the boy we're trying to cast . . . as if we plucked you right off the cover of the book. We've already picked the cast, or we thought we had, but we can write another person into the script, give him a line or two, and switch you to the role of Michael Madigan. It's a really good part. How about it?"

"I don't think so, mister. I'm no actor. I just came to see about my dog . . . kind of had my heart set on Newby being a star and everything."

"Storm, what if I said it's both of you . . . or neither one of you?"

"What if I'm no good at it? I've never done nothing like that before. Besides, you said you already picked the people. They wouldn't want me, I'm pretty sure."

"I like to think they want what's best for the play, Storm, and I've got a feeling that's you."

"You joshing me?"

"Couldn't be more serious."

"Just don't think so, mister."

"Well, if you don't trust my judgment, let's ask Newby what he thinks. One bark means yes. Two barks mean no."

"Do you think a *little* dog should be in this play, Newby?" Ben asked.

Newby looked around. Then he barked once.

"Do you want Storm to be in the play with you?"

Newby looked first at Ben, then back at Storm. He yipped once more.

"Wait till I get that dog home!" said Storm, smiling. "What does he know anyhow?"

"I thought you said Newby was smarter than most people you know," Ben said. "So what's it going to be. Is he dumb? Or smart?"

Storm broke into a wider smile.

"Then it's settled," Ben said. "We've got a show to put on in just over two weeks. Do you mind filling out this questionnaire before you go?"

"Like I said, mister, I don't read too good . . . don't write too good, neither."

"No problem. Kelly will ask you the questions and write down what you say."

Five minutes later, Carrie saw Ben open his briefcase and tuck Storm Sellers's answers on top of the stack. Then she sneaked out the door when she saw her mother's car pull up.

7

FROM BEN'S BRIEFCASE

QUESTIONS FOR THE CAST OF *CURTAIN CALL*

Name: Liza Barrett (two R's and two T's)

School/Grade: Brownsville Elementary, Mrs. Horne's fifth grade (gifted class)

Previous acting, singing, or dancing experience, if any: Five years of dancing lessons; singing in church choir; lead in class play (first, second, third, and fourth grade).

Sometimes actors have to play happy roles. Sometimes they need to act sad or angry. It helps many actors to imagine something that actually makes them feel that way. What can you think of that might make you happy? Sad? Angry?

Happy: Hearing people clap for me after a dance recital or seeing them smile after I have sung a solo at church.

Sad: Thinking about how I nearly missed winning the county spelling bee because I almost accidentally left out the "i" in "genius."

Angry: Jealous people who say mean things about me . . . like, that I get picked to do certain things just because my father owns the newspaper or my mother is PTA president.

QUESTIONS FOR THE CAST OF CURTAIN CALL

Name: Margaret Blake

School/Grade: Graduate of Yale School of Drama; numerous professional acting workshops; married with three grown children

Previous acting, singing, or dancing experience, if any: Over sixty plays, including summer stock, repertory, and off-Broadway. Understudy for Miss Hannigan in a national tour of *Annie*. This is my first role since I stopped acting to raise my children, and I am excited to be back onstage after a twenty-year recess!

Sometimes actors have to play happy roles. Sometimes they need to act sad or angry. It helps many actors to imagine something that actually makes them feel that way. What can you think of that might make you happy? Sad? Angry?

Happy: My first time onstage.

Sad: My last time onstage.

Angry: When my children tell me I'm too old to do something.

QUESTIONS FOR THE CAST OF *CURTAIN CALL*

Name: John Jeremy Jones, Jr. (Call me J.J.)

School/Grade: Homeschooled (fourth grade)

Previous acting, singing, or dancing experience, if any: I help my mother play the organ by turning the pages of music for her when she nods.

Sometimes actors have to play happy roles. Sometimes they need to act sad or angry. It helps many actors to imagine something that actually makes them feel that way. What can you think of that might make you happy? Sad? Angry?

Happy: When my dad lets me ring the church bells.

Sad: My mom crying (she's only cried once, I think).

Angry: When I do something bad and someone says I should know better because I'm a preacher's kid.

QUESTIONS FOR THE CAST OF CURTAIN CALL

Name: Ann McCarrity O'Connor. Carrie is short for the McCarrity part.

School/Grade: The Holcomb School, fifth grade

Previous acting, singing, or dancing experience, if any: Starring role in school play. I sang and danced and acted all at the same time.

Sometimes actors have to play happy roles. Sometimes they need to act sad or angry. It helps many actors to imagine something that actually makes them feel that way. What can you think of that might make you happy? Sad? Angry?

Happy: Thinking that Dad had to do another operation and couldn't get there in time to see my school play, then seeing him standing at the back door of the auditorium just before my part came on.

Sad: When my best friend, Holland, and her little sister, Allie, moved away.

Angry: When I think about the time I broke something special on Mom's desk. I got mad at myself for being so clumsy and mad at her for getting so mad at me for being so clumsy.

QUESTIONS FOR THE CAST OF *CURTAIN CALL*

Name: Storm Sellers (Yes, that really is my real name!)

School/Grade: Brownsville Elementary, fourth grade (second time)

Previous acting, singing, or dancing experience, if any: I hate that stuff.

Sometimes actors have to play happy roles. Sometimes they need to act sad or angry. It helps many actors to imagine something that actually makes them feel that way. What can you think of that might make you happy? Sad? Angry?

Happy: Swimming with Newby in the creek out back of my great-uncle's house; Newby has a fish in his mouth and is splashing me.

Sad: When Uncle Will sold his truck. He said he was too old to drive it anyway, but I know he loved that truck.

Angry: When Newby got caught in a raccoon trap and hurt his leg. I still think Old Man Presley set that trap because he said Newby chased his cows. That's why Uncle Will sold his truck—to pay the doctor who fixed Newby's leg.

––––––––

QUESTIONS FOR THE CAST OF *CURTAIN CALL*

Name: Matt Stamper, Jr.

School/Grade: Norman Elementary School (Norman, Florida), fourth grade

Previous acting, singing, or dancing experience, if any: Got called back for a hot dog ad, but didn't get the role (though I did get to ride in the Wienermobile).

Sometimes actors have to play happy roles. Sometimes they need to act sad or angry. It helps many actors to imagine something that actually makes them feel that way. What can you think of that might make you happy? Sad? Angry?

Happy: The thought of discovering a skateboarding park in Brownsville, where we come for summer vacations. I WISH!

Sad: When my father locked up my skateboard because I sassed my new stepmother. He said I couldn't have it back until I apologized and showed her some respect. Guess I won't be skateboarding around here for a while.

Angry: Leaving my friends in Florida to come here for the summer. Nothing to do!

———

QUESTIONS FOR THE CAST OF *CURTAIN CALL*

Name: Yonah Woods (P.S. Sometimes people call me Yo or Yo-Yo. I like to be called Yonah best.)

School/Grade: Brownsville Elementary, Mrs. Hurst's third grade

Previous acting, singing, or dancing experience, if any: Clogging at the county fair for four years; can call square dances pretty good; role of camel in the Christmas play at church.

Sometimes actors have to play happy roles. Sometimes they need to act sad or angry. It helps many actors to imagine something that actually makes them feel that way. What can you think of that might make you happy? Sad? Angry?

Happy: Listening to Grandpa Al tell how bad Daddy was when he was a boy.

Sad: Once this baby bird fell out of a tree in our front yard. We named him Lucky, and we tried to feed him, but he only lived two days. Mom said Lucky was still a good name for him, though, because he was lucky that we loved him so much while he was here.

Angry: When someone yells at their dog. If I could have a dog, I'd never be mean to it. Last Christmas, I asked for a dog, but I got a sister instead.

8

GETTING IT RIGHT

There was something Carrie just didn't like about Liza B-A-double-R-E-double-T. In fact, there wasn't one thing she *did* like.

She didn't like the way Liza bragged about her father's newspaper all the time. The whole newspaper wasn't even as long as one section of the *New York Times*. She didn't like the way Liza bragged about winning the county spelling bee three years in a row. "Can you spell 'obnoxious'?" Carrie could picture herself saying if Liza bragged one more time. And the way she treated Ben and Kelly, well, it was so syrupy nice it would make *anyone* sick.

Maybe Liza's clothes, Carrie decided. She *did* like them. They looked like something Carrie's friends back in New York would pick out. But clothes don't make the person, her mother had reminded her often when she had asked for another new outfit she knew she didn't need. In Liza's case, Carrie thought, that sure was true. And the way Liza had talked about the McCarrity family being so poor when they lived in Brownsville—well, Carrie *really* didn't like that.

So just who did Carrie see first when her mother stopped the car in front of the theater the next morning? Miss Double-R-double-T herself. "Now be nice," her mother said as if she could read Carrie's mind. Carrie slammed the door a little harder than usual, but not hard enough for her mother to make her come back and do it again properly.

"Bet you get the role of Michael Madigan's little sister," Liza said as they walked up the stairs. "My mother says that's what will probably happen . . . because your mother wrote the book and everything."

"I got a part in this play all by myself!" Carrie said, not nicely at all. "My mother didn't have anything to do with it."

Liza just smiled a fake little smile and opened the theater door. "I wonder who will be Michael Madigan?"

"I know," said Carrie, proud that she knew something Liza didn't.

"Bet you don't," Liza baited her.

"Do too," said Carrie.

"Then prove it. If you're wrong, I'll tell everyone that I know for a fact you got the role just because of your mother. But if you're right, then I'll tell everyone how you deserved it."

"Storm Sellers," Carrie said without really thinking. "He's got the role."

"He didn't even try out," said Liza. "And he couldn't possibly be in the play anyway. He can hardly even read."

"I'm telling you, Liza, Storm is Michael Madigan. And I know he can't read very well. Or write either. Kelly had to write his answers for him on that form we all had to fill out yesterday."

"How do you know?" Liza asked.

"I just do," said Carrie. She smiled a fake little smile right back at Liza when she said it.

Carrie could already hear voices when they walked inside. The theater was dark, except for the light spilling off the stage into the front rows. Ben was sitting on the stage steps talking to Kelly, and Kelly was jotting something down on her script. Carrie was close enough to see her pen glide across the page.

"All right. It's nine o'clock!" Ben yelled, clapping his hands. "Everybody on stage. We start on time, and we end . . . well, we end when we end." He laughed. "Act 1, Scene 1. Oh, I guess I forgot to tell you who plays what role. Anyone want to know?"

Everyone sat in silence, almost afraid to answer.

"Well, Mrs. Blake is the teacher. I guess that's no surprise. And, Liza, I want you to play Michael Madigan's little sister. You think you can handle that?"

"Thank you. I'd love to. I'll do my best," said Liza.

When Ben turned his head, Liza looked right at Carrie and faked a smile again. "Guess I was wrong about your mother after all," she whispered.

"And Michael Madigan? Drum roll, please, Kelly." Kelly began to drum on the stage. "The role of Michael Madigan will be played by . . . Storm Sellers."

Carrie looked right at Liza and faked a smile right back. "I guess I was right," she whispered.

"Storm wasn't here yesterday, but I know you'll all make him feel welcome," Ben said. "Come on down, Storm. Bring Newby, too." Everybody followed Ben's eyes to the back of the theater, where Storm was standing, Newby under his arm. He walked slowly toward the stage, taking off his baseball cap and tipping it when he passed Ben. Then he sat down by himself—across from where everyone else was sitting—and laid his cap across one knee and Newby across the other. Even in the darkness, Carrie could just feel that he was scared.

"Everybody else will play Michael's classmates," Ben continued. "Kelly will pass out the list of roles." Carrie ran her finger down her list until she saw her name. Claire, she thought. I'm Claire. She doesn't have many lines at all.

"Now we can start with Act 1, Scene 1," Ben said. "J.J., you start."

But after J.J. had read the first two lines, Ben called, "I can't hear you, J.J. Talk to the last row in the balcony."

"But we don't have a balcony," J.J. said.

"Then pretend we do," Ben said loudly, pointing to a space in the rafters. "Project!"

J.J. tried again, this time much louder.

"I didn't say scream," Ben commented with a smile. "I said *project*. Speak from your diaphragm. From your stomach, J.J. Take it again. From the top."

J.J. began again. His words came out just right. Not too soft. Not too loud.

"Now you've got the idea," Ben said. "Good for you!"

J.J. said his next two lines really fast.

"Slower, J.J., much slower," Ben yelled. "Just be-cause you say your lines loud doesn't mean you have to say them fast, too. Slow down. You're rushing them."

Poor J.J. started again.

"That's better," Ben called. "Remember to look at Liza. You should be talking to her, not to the audience."

Ben would have made a really great teacher, Carrie thought. He explained things so that everyone could understand the first time. "Now, J.J., you exit *stage right*"—he pointed to the part of the stage on the actor's right—"and, Matt, you exit *stage left.*" He pointed to the other side.

Carrie could tell that acting in this play was going to be harder than acting in *Nothing but the Tooth.* And she could tell that Ben knew a lot more about acting than her teacher, Mrs. Gregory, did.

"So the left side of the stage isn't really stage left?" Matt asked.

"That's *right*," Ben said. "I mean, you got that *right*." Ben laughed at his mistake. "So if I say, 'Exit stage right,' which way will you go, Yonah?"

Yonah pointed toward her right.

"Good job," said Ben.

"What if you don't know your left from your right . . . like Storm?" asked Liza. She laughed when she said it.

Ben glared at Liza. "That's quite enough, Liza," he said slowly.

Carrie had never heard anyone sound so strict. Not even her parents.

The woman who was going to be the teacher in the play went over and stood next to Storm. "Sometimes I still confuse my right with my left," Mrs. Blake said gently, looking at Storm. "And when I do, I just remember that left starts with L, and I form an L with my thumb and the finger next to it, like this." She took Storm's hand and showed him how to make the L. "If your L's going in the direction an L should go when it faces you, that's your left hand."

"Storm will get it all mixed up," Liza said. "He writes his letters backward all the time. I should know. I had to sit right beside him in the fourth grade, until I asked the teacher to move me because he smelled like . . . like yesterday's tuna fish sandwich." She laughed.

"You're the only one around here who stinks," Storm bellowed. "That's what you are. You're a spoiled, extra rotten, extra stinking brat!"

Liza swirled her hair and laughed. His words didn't seem to bother her at all.

"Well, at least I didn't have to ask Kelly to write my answers on that form we had to fill out yesterday," she said.

Carrie couldn't believe Liza had said that, especially in front of Ben. And she couldn't believe she had been the one to tell her. They were all getting off on the wrong foot, and it was as much her fault as it was Liza's. Maybe even more.

"One more word from you, Liza, and you won't be exiting stage right or stage left. You'll be exiting out the back door . . . for good!"

Ben wasn't yelling, but Carrie could tell he was very angry.

"And I mean it!" he said.

"But—"

Carrie's heart pounded as she anticipated Liza's next words, but Ben didn't let Liza finish the sentence.

"Not . . . one . . . more . . . word."

The stage grew quiet, except for the sputtering of a spotlight.

"Let's take a break," he finally said. He sounded calm, but he wasn't. "Five minutes."

Everyone exited stage right, where there were restrooms, benches, and a water fountain. Everyone except for Storm. He exited stage left and kept on going.

"You told, mister!" he yelled as he ran. Down the stage steps. Up the side aisle. Through the heavy doors that led onto the wide porch with the flapping flags on top. Newby was right behind him. Ben was hustling along just a few steps behind them both.

The door was heavy, and Storm needed both hands to heave it open. Ben caught the door before it closed and followed Storm out. Carrie could hear Ben's voice getting louder.

"But we need you, Storm! You're just right for this role. We need you."

"Well, I don't need this stupid play, mister. You heard her. I don't even know my left from my right. I'm not going back in there, and nobody can make me!"

Carrie could still hear Storm yelling after the door slammed shut.

She sat in silence, grateful for the darkness that kept her blush from showing. She couldn't even look at Liza. She had never felt worse in her whole life. Absolutely never. And there wasn't one thing she could do to take her words back. Not one thing!

Nobody spoke after Ben followed Storm out of the theater. Carrie wished the silence would swallow her up. It was the longest five minutes of her life.

Suddenly the overhead lights flashed in the theater.

"Okay, everybody, break's over," Kelly said. "I'll take over until Ben gets back. Have a seat."

"Thanks, but I've already got one," said J.J. He pointed to his backside.

Everybody waited to see if Kelly would laugh.

When she did, they laughed, too. Carrie was grateful for the laughter. Then Kelly pointed offstage to the front row of chairs. "Have a *chair*."

"How come I got the part of Louis the Loser?" asked Matt.

"We all know that you're nothing like Louis," said Kelly, "but you're such a good actor you can make people think you are."

Matt looked proud when she said it.

"We should finish blocking this play by tomorrow," Kelly began.

Blocking. So that's what they were doing. Another new word to learn, thought Carrie. By the time the play was over, she might know more about acting than anybody in her class at Holcomb. Maybe even more than Mrs. Gregory.

"What's 'blocking' mean?"

Carrie was glad Yonah had asked the question so she wouldn't have to.

" 'Blocking' means figuring out where everyone needs to be onstage. That's usually the first thing we do."

"What's the next thing?" Matt asked that.

"You start to learn your lines. You go over and over your role until you know it so well the audience will believe you actually are the character you're playing. Next you practice little scenes. Then you run through the whole play. Limp through it at first, really. Just to get an idea of how all the parts fit together."

"What's the next thing?" Liza asked that.

"Then you go off book. You should be ready to do that by this weekend."

"How do you go off book?" Liza again.

"That means you have to have your lines memorized so you don't read them from the script."

"What if someone forgets a line?"

"Just yell the word 'line,' Yonah, and I'll yell out the line you've forgotten to get you started again. It's no big deal. Everybody forgets a line now and then. You just have to keep on going. That's the number one rule in the theater. *No matter what happens, the show must go on.*" Suddenly she began to laugh. "I remember once when we were doing a show in a little theater in New York City. We were a few minutes into the second act of *King Lear* when a couple of people in the third row started jumping up. Then it happened in the fourth row. Then the fifth. We had no idea what was happening, but, as they say, the show must go on. We just kept saying our lines as if nothing had happened." By now Kelly was belly-laughing. "We found out after the show that a rat had made its way into the old theater and started rubbing up against people's legs, and that's what all the hopping was about!"

"What happened to the rat?" asked Yonah.

"It ran away, I guess," said Kelly, still laughing. "Probably never wanted to see another play."

Liza shuddered. Carrie guessed that she definitely didn't like hearing about rats.

"What if you forget a line during the play or get it all wrong?" Matt asked.

Carrie could tell that he was worried, too, even if he was such a great actor.

"You have to trust the other actors to help you out. That's why you've got to learn to listen so hard onstage. Because if another actor makes a mistake, you've got to know the last thing he said so you can help him out. You can't be thinking about who's in the audience or how your hair looks. You've got to focus really hard on what's being said and forget about everything else. In the theater, we call that 'living in the moment.'"

Carrie thought she understood.

"There's another thing we say in the theater: If you're too afraid to do it wrong, you'll never get it right. You've got to loosen up—to experiment until you figure out how to become your character. That's what rehearsals are for." She looked at each actor as she said it.

"And there are a few other things I want you to keep in mind," Kelly said.

"Such as?"

"You're in charge of your own props. Never, ever

touch a prop that isn't yours. You might put it somewhere else by mistake, and the actor who needs it might not be able to find it."

"I knew someone who had to duel with a broomstick because someone had moved his sword," said Mrs. Blake. "Looked pretty silly on stage, he did, cutting the air with a broomstick. And speaking of swords, I saw an actor actually get cut onstage during a duel. Not a bad cut, really, but deep enough to draw blood."

"Did they stop the play?"

"Remember what Kelly said. No matter what, the show must go on. The actor just mopped at the cut with his shirttail and went right back onstage . . . blood and all. Nobody in the audience even knew he'd been hurt. They thought the blood was fake."

Carrie couldn't imagine being cut by a sword and not yelling. She always yelled *ouch* when D.D. took a splinter out of her finger—even before the needle had pricked her skin. She never knew being an actress would be this hard.

"Will we get to use fake blood?" asked Matt.

Carrie could tell he wanted to.

"I'm sorry, but nobody in *Curtain Call* bleeds."

"Maybe instead of a sore throat, he could get cut real bad. I think blood would be better," suggested J.J.

"No blood," said Kelly. "Sorry!"

"Anything else we need to know?" asked Liza.

She didn't seem worried about what had happened to Storm at all. Nobody did, actually.

"There's another rule in the theater. Never correct another actor. Never! That's the director's job, and nobody does it better than Ben Sanders. By the way, I hope you all appreciate who Ben Sanders is."

"Who is he?"

"Let me put it this way. Ben is one of the best directors there is, if you ask me. He usually works in big theaters on Broadway."

Carrie thought of the noisy New York street not too far from her apartment. Why, one block on Broadway had more lights than all the houses in Brownsville. Maybe in all of North Carolina. Broadway seemed awfully far off to her right now. Suddenly, Carrie wished she were still in New York . . . or anywhere else in the world but Brownsville . . . someplace where nobody would ever find out that *she* had told about Kelly's writing Storm's answers on the questionnaire for him.

"Ben has worked with some of the finest actors in the business," Kelly continued, "and he always manages to get the best from each one. He wanted to do this play in Brownsville because his parents still live here and he knew coming home to direct a play would make them proud. Besides, he absolutely *loves* the Michael Madigan books. He has wanted to turn *Curtain Call* into a play for a long time."

Carrie felt a little better when she said that.

Kelly looked up and down the front row to be sure everyone was listening. "Actors all over the world would love to be in your shoes right now," she said. "You're lucky to be working with Ben Sanders. As a matter of fact, I'm lucky to be working with him, too."

Carrie heard the soft *whoosh* of the back door closing and saw Ben walk out of the shadows and into the light of the stage. He was alone.

Kelly set her promptbook on the edge of the stage. "Where's Storm?" she asked.

Ben shrugged his shoulders. "Gone," he said, looking at Liza.

Carrie knew that he should really have been looking at someone else.

9

A Lot to Look Back On

"I don't like this place. And I don't like these people, either. And I never want to be in a play again as
long as I live."

Carrie's words spilled out the second she had
climbed into the car and shut the door. Today, her
mother was reading a book while she waited in the
car for rehearsal to end. She sandwiched a gum
wrapper between the pages to mark her place before
she slid the book back into her purse.

This whole mess is partly my mother's fault, Carrie thought. If she had been on time like this yesterday, I wouldn't have had to stay late and overhear
Storm's conversation with Ben.

"Am I invited to your pity party?"

Carrie hated it when her mother said that. It made her feel like such a baby.

"But this is really serious, Mom. The star of the show just quit, so we don't even have anyone to play Michael Madigan. And what's even worse, he took his dog with him. And you know better than anybody that Michael Madigan never went anywhere without his dog."

"They'll find another dog, Carrie. And another Michael. You'll see. Things like that happen in the theater all the time."

"Ben said the other dogs that tried out barked all the time or ran off or sniffed at everything instead of paying attention. One almost won a tug-of-war with the curtain." She let out a deep breath. "And I'm not even Michael Madigan's little sister. I'm just some dumb girl in his class who doesn't get to say anything."

"Well, Michael Madigan wasn't always all that nice to his little sister anyway," Mrs. O'Connor said. That was one of the most irritating things about her mother. She found something good about absolutely everything. "Today's troubles are tomorrow's triumphs," she had said to Carrie at least a million times. She said it again, as if on cue.

"I bet I never feel triumphant about this!" She punctuated her words with something that sounded halfway between a sob and a sigh. She wished she could tell her mother how it was all her fault, about how she had been sneaky enough to overhear Ben talk Storm into being in the play, about how she had even been stupid enough to tell Liza what she knew. But she just couldn't bear for her mother to know. At least not now.

"There's something I want you to see," her mother said, starting the car. "I've been waiting for the right time to show it to you. I think that time might be now."

"You promise we'll be back by three for the next rehearsal?" Carrie asked as her mother twisted their rented Ford around first one curve, then another. "I can't be late."

"You won't be. I promise."

Carrie could feel her stomach swim with every hairpin turn. She had never seen anything like what she saw on the mountain road they were traveling.

An old dog slept on the steps leading to a double-wide trailer that housed Betty's Beauty Bazaar. That's what the little wooden sign out front said. Carrie counted twenty gigantic satellite dishes beside weathered farmhouses and quaint summer cottages as they climbed the mountain. Cables can't be run this high up, her mother explained. Carrie counted more than a dozen statues of deer, some brightly painted, some stone gray. She had never seen those in New York, either. In fact, the closest

Carrie had ever come to deer was in the movie *Bambi*. "You think we might see a real deer?" Carrie asked at last, her words breaking the peaceful silence inside the car.

"Probably . . . before we leave," her mother said. "These mountains are full of them."

Carrie looked at her mother's hair, gathered loosely into a ponytail and fastened with a yellow scrunchie. She had never seen her wear it that way before in New York, except when she pulled it back to put cream on her face. Carrie thought the ponytail made her mother look younger. Something about her mother's face looked different, too. More relaxed maybe. Her book must be going well, she thought. Not as many balled-up pieces of paper as usual in the wastebasket back at the hotel room. That was always a good sign. Carrie wished her own life were going as well.

"Are we almost there?"

"Almost."

"Where are we going anyway? You never told me."

"It's a surprise."

They stopped in front of a crumbling house and got out. The house was two stories high, and the wood structure had swayed to one side. "This is where we used to live when I was your age," her mother said at last. A few patches of paint formed strange shapes on mostly bare wood. Bushy flowers bordered the sagging front porch. A swing on the porch creaked a singsong in the breeze.

"I didn't know if the old house would still be here, but I wanted to come back anyway. Doesn't look like anybody's lived here in years," Mrs. O'Connor said, bending over to smell a flower. She brushed the petals against her face. "I remember when my mother planted these," she said, far off in thought. "I thought she said she was planting 'penny bushes' instead of 'peony bushes.' Was I ever disappointed when they only bloomed pink and white blossoms!" She laughed. "We could have used a few extra pennies back then."

Carrie followed her mother through the open front door. Her mother had to push cobwebs away to get inside.

"I don't think anybody could ever fix this up again," said Carrie. "Why don't they just tear the old place down?"

"Guess whoever owns it now figures one good windstorm, and it will fall down by itself." She paused. "This was our living room," she said, rubbing her hand along a mantel. "Come here, Carrie." She guided her daughter's fingers across something cut into the wood on the underside of the mantel. "My father made this mantel out of the trunk of an old tree the wind had blown down. It was a Christmas present for my mother. I watched him plane the slab of wood. Sand it. Paint it white, out behind the barn where nobody could see him working. He let me watch him nail it in place as a surprise for my mother when she came home from choir practice."

Carrie kept rubbing her fingers across the bottom of the mantel.

"My brother had gotten a new pocketknife for Christmas that year, and for some reason I'm not even sure he knew, he carved his initials on the underneath part with it. I came in the room and caught him. He said if I ever told on him, he'd swear he heard me say forty different curse words on the school bus."

"Did you?"

"Probably not forty. But I did say a word or two I shouldn't have." She laughed. "Of course, I had learned them from my brother."

"So you never told about his initials?"

"No. I wouldn't have even if Clay hadn't threatened me. Anytime he got in trouble, I ended up crying more than he did." She laughed again and shook her head. "If Clay wasn't happy, then I wasn't happy either."

Carrie had never heard her mother talk much about Clay before. D.D. had told her that something had happened to him when her mother was little, and that her mother would tell her about it when Carrie was older. Carrie guessed she was old enough now. Mrs. O'Connor took Carrie's fingers and guided them across the thick coat of dust covering the front window. She wrote Carrie's initials in sweeping cursive letters. A.M.O. Ann McCarrity O'Connor.

"It's odd what you remember, coming back to a place." Her mother kept on writing initials, straining until she couldn't reach any higher. "The night after Clay fell through the ice on the pond out back and drowned was the coldest night I ever remember. It was snowing, and I asked my father if I could go outside and set off a sparkler I had saved from the Fourth of July. I waved it around, writing my name in the air first and then Mom's name, and then Dad's. And then I wrote Clay's. I wondered if it was still okay to write his name, now that he was gone, but I didn't ask anybody. I remember that I put the sparkler in the snow and watched the white snowbank snuff the glow out . . . I remember thinking that was just how I felt . . . as if with my brother gone, all the glow had been snuffed out of me, too."

Carrie watched as her mother shuddered a little and then stood up straight, even straighter than usual. Carrie followed her up the stairs, which seemed to moan under their steps.

"This was my room," Mrs. O'Connor said, walking into the smallest bedroom Carrie had ever seen. She walked around the edges, brushing back a curtain that was rotting at the window, and continued down the hall. "This was Clay's room." It was a little larger, but not much. "I remember being afraid to go into his room after he drowned. I didn't want anybody to take his baseball posters off the wall or touch his clothes. I wanted everything to stay exactly the way it had been." The walls were bare now, the paint peeling and mildewed.

Then they entered a bathroom off the center hall. "This was always the scene of our worst fights. Clay always fogged up the mirror and used up all the hot water with his showers, and he left great globs of toothpaste drool caked on the sink and wet towels on the floor. And if I complained about it, which I almost always did, he'd chase me down the hall, popping me with a towel and yelling that I could have first dibs when I was the oldest." Mrs. O'Connor ran her fingers along the inside of the sink. A leaky faucet had, over so many years, worn a river of brown rust into the middle of the basin. She tried to turn the handle, but no water came out. The faucet only squeaked in a spooky sort of way. "I remember thinking when Clay died that I was the oldest now and I could take a shower anytime I wanted to. But it wasn't the same as having first dibs. I even missed the soppy towels he had always left on the floor."

Carrie followed her mother out of the bathroom and down the stairs, making a sharp right into the kitchen. A chimney pipe stuck out of the wall where a stove had once stood. An old sink was still in place, but one handle was missing. "This is where my mother made the world's best potato soup— she always left the skin on the potatoes before she souped them—and where we made valentines for everyone in my class. My mother—your grand-mother—always made me go up and down the rows a dozen times in my mind to be sure we hadn't left anyone out."

The back door was already open, and they walked down an overgrown path to a dilapidated shed. "We kept some chickens in here, and Dad would milk Moo in this stall every morning before breakfast."

"Moo?" Carrie said. "Now that's original, Mom."

She laughed. "I named all the animals around here . . . the fish in the pond, even the birds that came to feed. And yes, I named Moo." Her mother seemed almost proud of the name. "We had so much work to do on the farm, Carrie, but I just loved this place. When I had finished my chores, I could go outside and sing softly to the chickens or quack back at the ducks. Sometimes, my friends would come over, and we'd build elaborate club-houses out of hay bales. Sometimes, I would sit on the fence and tell stories to Moo."

"Whatever happened to Moo?"

"They came and took her when we lost the farm.

We didn't have much, but the bank took all we had, except for the clothes on our backs and a few boxes of things we could carry and Clay's old dog, Dory. Of course, the dog wasn't worth much to anybody but Clay. She meant the world to him."

"Were you *really* poor?"

Carrie remembered what Liza's mother had said about her mother's growing-up days, about how her family was even too poor to buy pencils and paper for school. She hoped it wasn't true.

"I remember asking my mother that the night before we moved. I was sitting with her in the old rocker on the front porch, swaying back and forth, and I just up and asked her, 'Are we poor?' "

"What did she say?"

"She said as long as she had a child to rock with, she'd never feel poor. And I remember something else about our last night on the farm. I finally got up the courage to tell her something I'd been worrying about ever since Clay had drowned. I was so scared that something would happen to my father and her. But she promised me she would stay around as long as she possibly could . . . said she wanted to read the books I was going to write someday. I'm glad she did get to read some of them, just as she promised, though not as many as I would have liked."

Carrie didn't really remember her grandparents—they both had died when she was still a toddler—

but she somehow felt close to them right now. She felt close to her mother, too, as if her mother thought Carrie was finally grown up enough to hear some things that were really difficult to talk about.

"So you knew even then that you wanted to be a writer when you grew up?" It was the only thing Carrie could think of to say.

Her mother nodded. "I've always liked to keep company with words." She looked right at Carrie. "I've tried to keep company with the ones that are helpful, not hurtful."

Carrie whacked at the weeds around the house with an old board she had picked up at the barn. She tried not to think of the hurtful words she had uttered at Storm's expense.

"No offense, Mom, but I can't see why anybody would want to be a writer. Writing seems so hard sometimes, even for you."

"I guess everybody wants to carve initials into some kind of mantel," said her mother quietly as she stooped to pluck a white peony from its stem. She held it to her face and breathed in deeply, then handed it to Carrie. "For me, there's not another mantel in the world more important than one built with words."

Carrie slipped her little hand into her mother's bigger one, gently rubbing the fingers that had fashioned so many words, marveling at the mystery of where her mother had come from and what she had chosen to do with her life. And for the first time, Carrie thought she understood. "Were you always a good writer?" she asked at last.

"I wrote my first book when I was not much older than you are. It wasn't very good, but I was so proud of it."

"Do you still have it?"

"My mother saved it. It's around somewhere."

"May I see it?"

"We'll see," her mother said, but Carrie knew by her mother's smile that the answer was really yes.

10

CLEANING UP THE MESS

They sang Carrie's tooth song all the way down the mountain, past the cement deer and stone toadstools, past Betty's Beauty Bazaar, past Big Joe's Drive-In, where they had stopped for boxed barbecue chicken on the way up the mountain, all the way to the Apple Barn Theater. Ben was walking up the driveway just as the clock on the square chimed a quarter to three. Mrs. O'Connor honked and waved him to the window. Carrie hoped he wouldn't say anything about what had happened that morning. Then Carrie realized that Ben couldn't say anything because he didn't even know she had been in the theater—and he never *would* know unless Liza told him . . . or unless Carrie herself did.

"So how's it feel coming home to Brownsville again?" Mrs. O'Connor asked as Ben poked his head through the open window and kissed her on the cheek.

"It seemed like a good idea at the time," he said, laughing a little. "But I think I'm more nervous about opening in Brownsville than on Broadway. I'm glad Carrie's going to be in the play, though I really had no idea she was your daughter."

"She wanted it that way. She likes to do things all by herself."

Carrie wished they would stop talking about her.

"You don't have a son you could loan us, do you? We're minus one Michael Madigan."

"Wish I did. Carrie told me the boy you had picked was perfect for the role. Said he looked just like she had always pictured Michael Madigan. Can't you think of a way to get him to come back?"

"I doubt it. I tried. Storm's as proud as Will Sellers, his uncle . . . or his great-uncle, or his great-great-uncle, I'm not sure which. I wonder how old that man is. He seemed absolutely ancient even when we were kids. What was it we called him? Santa Sellers? I remember how he and his wife always decorated that truck of his for the Christmas parade—called it Santa Sellers's Sleigh. It always won first place in the float division."

"Of course, it was probably the *only* float in the

parade," Mrs. O'Connor said. "Why's Storm living with his uncle?"

"The grapevine around here says Will Sellers broke both legs falling from a barn he was roofing . . . just about the time Storm's father died. Storm's mother sent him here for the summer to take care of his Uncle Will . . . thought the change would be good for him. That was a year ago. He liked the old man. Liked the mountains. Never went back to Charlotte, though his mother comes here to visit him when she can." Ben shook a pebble out of his shoe and checked his watch again.

"I can't quite figure it out," Ben said. "He reads just like a first-grader, pointing his finger at every word before he says it. But he's got a memory like an elephant. Last night, I worked with him on some lines. I'd say some and he'd throw them right back to me, word for word. All he has to do is hear a line once or twice, and it's his. He's plenty smart. I'm sure of that."

"People can be smart in different ways," said Mrs. O'Connor. "Let's hope he gets a teacher who is right for him."

"That's what he needs," Ben agreed. "A teacher like Mrs. McCabe. She was the one who made the difference in my life. Everyone deserves a teacher like that." He looked across the car at Carrie. "I guess I shouldn't be talking in front of you, should I?"

"It's okay. I won't say anything," she answered. Carrie felt sorry for Storm. Yonah had said she felt sorry for him, too. "I'm glad he's got Newby. That dog really loves him. You can just tell," Carrie said. "And that's the smartest dog I've ever seen."

"Which brings us to another problem. I've got Kelly out looking for a dog to take Newby's place right now, but from what I saw at auditions, I'm not too hopeful. No Lassies in the bunch, that's for sure. They either showed the manners of a junkyard hound or slinked off the stage as scared as a skunk caught in headlights."

"Have you thought about calling one of those professional dog trainers you use on Broadway? Maybe they could ship a dog to you."

"I don't want to do that," Ben said. "My father says that everything a person really needs is right here in these mountains." He looked at Carrie and smiled. "Don't worry, Carrie. We need *you* in the play. You may be a *daughter* of New York, but you're a *granddaughter* of these mountains."

Ben's words made Carrie feel proud.

"Maybe I could talk to Storm," Carrie suggested suddenly.

"You had nothing to do with it, Carrie," Ben said kindly. "I'm not sure anybody could make him change his mind. He thinks I told the cast he couldn't write the answers to his own questionnaire.

I can't figure out how Liza knew about that. Nobody but Kelly was in the theater when I was talking to Storm yesterday. I'll find out. The truth will come out sooner or later."

Carrie gulped. She hoped this truth wouldn't come out until much, much later—when she was about as ancient as Will Sellers.

"The truth always does come out, doesn't it," Mrs. O'Connor agreed.

The clock began to chime three times as Carrie followed Ben into the theater.

Ben had asked Liza to stay after rehearsal, and Carrie lingered just inside the open door, hoping to hear what he had to say to her. She knew she shouldn't stick around where they couldn't see her—her snooping was getting to be a habit—but Carrie just couldn't help herself. After all, if Liza was about to get in trouble, Carrie couldn't think of anything she'd rather witness. And if Liza was about to blame her, well, Carrie needed to know that, too. Maybe she could think up some way to convince her mother to go back to New York—before Ben could tell her what Carrie had done.

"Storm has more natural talent than anyone I've seen in a long time," Ben said to Liza, "though I can't get him to believe that yet. I've tried to talk to him, but I don't think he'll change his mind unless you apologize and ask him back yourself. I'm not sure he'd do it even then."

Liza was silent.

"I was just kidding around with him," she finally said. "Kids tease each other all the time. It's no big deal."

"I know *kids* say mean things to each other all the time," Ben began, "and maybe someday you'll realize how much words can hurt. But I'm not talking about *kids*, Liza. I'm talking about *actors*. I've worked with a lot of child actors—the best in the business—and I've never expected any less of them than I do of the adults in the cast. I can always judge a cast by the respect they show for one another. In my plays, they either get along"—he paused and looked Liza squarely in the eyes—"or they get out. I don't like what happened between you and Storm Sellers this morning one bit," Ben said calmly. His voice was firm. His brow was furrowed.

"I was just politely pointing out . . . just to be helpful . . . that Storm sometimes has trouble telling his left from his right." Liza stared at her feet to keep from looking at Ben. "And I suggested . . . just to be helpful . . . that it would be nice if he smelled a little better sometimes. Then he just exploded like he always does and called me a spoiled rotten, stinking brat—an extra spoiled rotten, extra stinking brat—those were his exact words."

"You may know your *right* from your *left*," Ben said, "but you don't seem to know a *right* from a *wrong*. You owe him an apology. If you want to be in this play, you'll find Storm and convince him to come back. Clean up the mess you've made. That's only fair."

Carrie's heartbeat quickened, and her throat felt raspy as she mustered up the courage to speak.

"It's not just Liza's fault," she said, a little louder than a whisper.

Ben noticed her standing in the doorway.

"I was still in the theater when you asked Storm to fill out that questionnaire, and I was stupid enough to tell Liza about it."

There was a long silence. She wished Ben would say something, but he didn't.

"I wish I could just . . . just . . . just kick my hurtful words all the way back to New York."

"And if I had to fill out the questionnaire about what makes me *sad*, I might have to consider what went on this morning," Ben said.

What he said didn't make Carrie feel any better, but at least he had finally said *something*. Then he was quiet again.

"I could go with Liza to see Storm," Carrie said,

trying to blot out the silence. "Maybe if the *two* of us apologized . . ."

Carrie left her sentence unfinished.

Ben nodded. "You took the words right out of my mouth," he said.

Mr. Barrett's Cadillac and Mrs. O'Connor's rented Ford slid into the parking lot at just about the same time, and Mrs. O'Connor got out. Carrie heard Liza tell her father through the car window that she needed to find Storm Sellers right away. "There's not a phone at Uncle Will's," she said, "and there's something Ben forgot to tell him about the play. I said I'd take care of it for him, he's so busy and everything."

Liza *is* a good actress, Carrie thought, the way she can lie and not even get caught. Maybe Ben was right to cast Liza as Michael's little sister. The time Carrie had told her mother the lie about breaking that picture frame, her mother knew it right away. Her mother said she had fibbed, but when her father heard about it later, he said there wasn't any use trying to dress up a lie by calling it something else. Carrie knew she'd eventually tell both her parents about what she had done that morning—about her hurtful words and everything. She suddenly realized that she wouldn't feel good again until she had confessed to her mother, just as she had done to Ben. But first, she had some serious work to do.

Mr. Barrett said he just couldn't *believe* Storm was in the play, but he'd be more than happy to drive her to Uncle Will's, if that would be a help to Ben.

"May Carrie go with me?" Liza asked Mrs. O'Connor ever so sweetly, as if nothing were wrong at all.

Carrie rolled her eyes. Her mother had once said that rolling the eyes was a close cousin to an outright sass. She hoped her mother hadn't seen her roll them.

"I think that's a fine idea," Mr. Barrett said. After he had realized who Mrs. O'Connor was, Mr. Barrett had sounded almost as nice as Liza.

"Sure. I'm glad Carrie is making some friends in Brownsville," Mrs. O'Connor said.

She didn't even ask me if I wanted to go, Carrie thought. Carrie didn't want to go *anywhere* with Liza, let alone to Storm Sellers's house. But she knew it was the least she could do.

They followed a stream all the way up the mountain. A sliver of moon appeared in the sky just as they came to an old farmhouse that looked almost like the one she had visited that afternoon with her mother, only a bit less run-down. Out front, a tractor tire framed some flowers; they weren't peonies, but they were a pretty pink. Two hens snuggled near the mailbox by the road. They flapped their wings and scattered when the car stopped.

Mr. Barrett started to get out of the car, but Liza stopped him. "We can do this all by ourselves," she said, giving Carrie another fake smile.

The girls walked down a short path to the front porch.

"This is all your fault. I don't want to do this," Liza said suddenly. "We don't have to go. We could just tell Ben that Storm slammed the door on us. I could make him believe us. Or we could tell him his old uncle went plum crazy and started screaming. Ben couldn't expect us to apologize when someone's shouting at us. He'd have to believe us if we both said it was true."

"I'll do the talking," Carrie said.

"That's only fair. It was your talking that started the whole mess anyway."

"Hello? Storm, are you there?" Carrie yelled through cupped hands.

A door screeched open. Storm Sellers poked his head through the crack.

"Don't come around here yelling," he said softly. "My uncle's asleep. Gets up early. Goes to bed early. It's his way." He gently pushed Newby away from the door with his foot and started to go back inside.

"Liza and I came to tell you we were sorry about what happened," Carrie said in a whisper, sticking her foot between the door and its frame. "Everyone's sorry, and everyone wants you to come back." She nudged Liza when she said it. Liza nodded enthusiastically.

"If you'll come back, my dad will put your name in the newspaper," Liza added. "In real big type. Why, the whole town will know you are the star of the play."

"Nobody I care about reads his old newspaper anyway," said Storm, "and you yourself said I couldn't read it."

Carrie felt the punch of his words.

"Then maybe I could get him to put your picture in real big. You'd like that, wouldn't you, Storm?"

He tried to shut the door again, but Carrie slid her foot farther through the crack. The summer air was thick with a long spell of nothing.

"There must be something we could say to change your mind," Carrie said.

"It's made up."

"If you could just see your way to do this for me, maybe you could think of something I could do for you . . . or maybe for Uncle Will." Liza glanced past the door and into the house when she said it.

Storm looked up. Silence again.

"There might be something," he said finally.

Liza came closer, but not too close. "What is it, Storm?"

Storm hesitated. "Help me figure out a way I could get my uncle's truck back. I tried to get the man at the junkyard to let me work it out by mowing his grass, but he said he liked to mow it himself."

Liza looked at him in disbelief. "You mean that old truck he always used to drive to town? What would he want it for anyway, Storm? Your uncle's way too old to drive, and you're way too young."

"I think he'd just like to have it around here again. Always said he'd be right proud to give it to me someday. Wanted me to have it as a present." He shrugged. "Said he just wanted to give me a simple gift." He stooped down to pat Newby when he said it.

"I'll think of something," said Carrie. "If you'll be in the play, I'll see what I can do."

"Uncle Will's real old, you know, and he's never taken nothing from nobody yet."

Carrie nodded at Storm's words, as if she understood.

"You'd have to figure out something so he wouldn't be ashamed to take it back."

"We'll think of something good," Carrie said. "I promise."

"So that's all? We get your uncle's truck back, and you'll be in the play?" Liza sounded puzzled.

"I'd do most anything to get that truck back . . . 'cept something that would make him 'shamed of me. You ever wanted something for someone else so bad you'd do almost anything to get it?" he asked.

Both girls looked first at each other, and then at the cracks in the porch floor. Neither one answered him.

"I did something that would make my parents ashamed," Carrie said softly, still trying not to look at him. "I was sort of hiding in the back of the theater when Ben was talking to you yesterday, and I told Liza about how you had trouble filling out that form."

"So it wasn't Ben that told on me?" Storm asked.

Carrie shook her head. "It was me, and I'm so sorry I did it."

"And I'm sorry for what I said, too," said Liza convincingly. Carrie couldn't tell whether she was lying or not.

"You're the sorriest-looking folks I've seen around here in a long time," said Storm. "I guess I'm supposed to say I'm sorry about how I tried to put glue in your chair at school." Storm looked straight at Liza.

Carrie remembered then what she'd heard Liza

say before the audition—about something that had happened at school.

"And about how I told the class I'd just given you something else to be stuck up about."

He wasn't exactly apologizing, but there was something in the way he said it that made Liza laugh—a real laugh, not fake. Carrie couldn't help but laugh, too.

"You reckon we could all just start over, Storm?" Carrie asked. *Reckon*. She was surprised at how quickly she had come to make the mountain words her own.

"I reckon," said Storm.

Carrie stuck out her hand, and Storm shook it awkwardly. "Then it's a deal," she said.

"Deal," said Storm.

"You won't chicken out about being in the play, will you?" asked Liza.

"Nope. Some say it's harder to face an audience than to wrestle a mountain lion. I'm not afraid of neither, really." Storm sounded proud when he said it.

"Rehearsal's at nine tomorrow. You'll be there, won't you? We all really do need you, Storm."

This time when Liza said it, Carrie could tell she wasn't lying.

"We keep our word" was all he said.

Liza and Carrie walked back to the car in moonlight. "I never dreamed so much could depend on an old truck," Liza said softly.

Even in the darkness, Carrie could see that most of the stuck-up-ness had been siphoned out of her.

Just a simple gift, Carrie kept saying to herself as she felt rocks poking up underneath her shoes. *Just a simple gift.*

11

SOMETHING TO REMEMBER ME BY

The seven actors—plus Newby—were quieter than usual on opening night. A few feet down the hall from the backstage door, they waited in a space called the greenroom—though the walls were washed with yellow, not green. "That is where the waiting takes place," Kelly had explained. The actors mingled around the bulletin board. An article from the morning edition of *Mountain Views* was pinned too high for little Yonah to see it, even if she stood on tiptoes, so Kelly took it down and cleared her throat. "We made front page again," she said. "Let's see what they said about us this time."

MICHAEL MADIGAN'S
CURTAIN CALL TO OPEN TONIGHT!

ALL PERFORMANCES SOLD OUT!

All Work (And Some Play!)

By Mary Lou McCune
Special Correspondent to *Mountain Views*

The Fourth of July celebration will begin a day early for the three hundred people lucky enough to have tickets for tonight's opening performance of *Michael Madigan's Curtain Call* at the Apple Barn Theater. "This is the biggest thing to happen to Brownsville since the state clogging championship twenty years ago," said Mayor Richard King. "Why, even Senator Jack Hunter called me about getting tickets."

Award-winning Broadway director L. Bennett Sanders says his cast will be ready when the curtain opens, with the author of the book on which the play is based seated in the front row. "I haven't watched any of the rehearsals," said Kate McCarrity O'Connor. "I can't wait to see how the characters pop off the pages of my book and become real."

Stage manager Kelly Clemens, who helped Sanders write the script, says the play is true to the book. "There are too many Michael Madigan fans out there for us to make many changes," she said.

For J. J. Jones, the hardest part was memorizing his lines. "I'd think about them when I went to bed at night and when I got up in the morning," he said. "I haven't missed one in a week."

Yonah Woods said memorizing wasn't that hard for her. "But I've only got to remember three lines," she said.

For Storm Sellers, who stars as Michael Madigan, the greatest surprise was the set. "I came in one day and there was this gigantic tree growing right out of the stage," he said. "The scenery looks like houses in a real town. You could almost climb the mountains in the background, they look so real."

Matt Stamper, Jr., said learning his dance

steps was the hardest part. "But I think skateboarding has helped me get coordinated," he said, "and my stepmother helped me practice, too."

Carrie O'Connor, daughter of Kate McCarrity O'Connor, admitted that being in a real play was more difficult than she thought. "I've never worked so hard in my entire life," she said.

Liza Barrett said she hoped their hard work would pay off. "There are an awful lot of people counting on us to be good."

For Margaret Blake, who has the role of the children's teacher, this play has reminded her why she loves acting. "It's not the smell of the makeup or the roar of the crowd," she said. "It's the people you get to work with. I am supposed to be the teacher in the play, but my students have taught me so much. They *all* deserve an A+ for effort."

According to Sanders, most directors prefer working with professional child actors instead of regular kids, but he has no regrets about picking his cast from the fifty children with connections to Brownsville who auditioned for him. "Every one of them could have contributed something to the play," he said. "I'm delighted at how these 'regular kids' have become true actors. They have risen to every challenge. They are *absolutely awesome!*"

The Apple Barn Theater says ticket sales have been absolutely awesome, too. The play, which runs through July 10, is completely sold out.

"Look at that big picture of Storm and Newby," Kelly said. "Neat stuff, huh?"

Storm smiled when he looked at it.

Kelly pinned the article back on the bulletin board. "And speaking of neat stuff"—she made a sound like a trumpet—"it's time for the loot."

She unlocked the door to an office right off the greenroom, and there on a desk were vases of flowers and a stack of shoe boxes with everyone's name on them. Kelly had told them earlier that, on opening night, actors sometimes get flowers from their families and usually give all the other cast members a little gift, something to remember them by. She had been collecting the presents secretly all day.

Liza had red roses in her vase. Carrie saw her name on a vase with gigantic pink and white blossoms in it. She opened the card. "Love from the 'penny bush'" was written in her mother's neat handwriting.

"Storm, you've got *five* bunches of flowers!" Kelly announced. Carrie knew her mother had sent him a bouquet because she was afraid nobody else would think to do so. She guessed the other parents had done the same thing.

Carrie took her cardboard box and fingered each item carefully. There was a yo-yo from Yonah. The card tied to the string said, "Only ups, no downs tonight. Love, Yonah." J.J. had painted everyone's name on a small lightbulb. "Let your little light shine," his card read. Matt Stamper's was really original. He had pasted a one-cent stamp on a piece of construction paper and written "+er" beside it. "Don't you get it?" he said, obviously disappointed. "Stamp-er." Everyone laughed. "Look what's on the back," said Liza. The words "Special Delivery" had been inked on it. "The man at the post office did it for me so it would look official," Matt said proudly.

Liza had given everyone a tiny doll's leg with "Break a leg" written on one side and her name on the other. "Break a leg" was theater talk for "good luck," Kelly had told them. Storm gave everyone a wooden star—about the size of a saucer. His uncle had whittled them, and everyone's name was carved on one of the points—even Newby's. Storm had done that himself after he checked with Mrs. Blake to be sure all the letters were just right. He had wanted to write something else in the center of the star, but he had run out of time. Mrs. Blake gave everyone a piece of chalk. The note tied around it said, "For my honor roll students." Newby gave a dog biscuit to everyone. His name was written on one side of the biscuit with a red magic marker. Carrie thought she recognized Kelly's handwriting, but she couldn't be sure.

Carrie waited for everyone to open her remembrance. It was rolled into a scroll and tied with a blue ribbon. For each cast member, Carrie had painted a picture of a mountain with the watercolors she had bought at the general store on the corner. Nine stick figures of people and one of a dog were climbing together to the top. Her mother had helped her think of the idea, but Carrie had done the painting all by herself.

"I'm gonna frame mine," Yonah said.

"It's almost time," Kelly said. "Ben wants to talk to you backstage."

The actors trooped from the greenroom to where their director was waiting. He gathered the cast around him in a tight knot.

"Tonight isn't about us," he began almost in a whisper. "It's about them." He pointed to the audience beyond the curtain. "Someone out there might feel like a Louis the Loser right now. Do your best

. . . for him." He looked around the circle slowly, staring each person in the eye. "Maybe there's also someone in those seats who doesn't need to be so selfish." Liza looked at Carrie, and she smiled, but it wasn't fake at all. "This play can show them how to think about others." He paused again. "Maybe people out there just need to laugh. Do your best for those people, too. Give them *all* your best gifts. Give them *something great to remember you by.* I've seen you do it! I *know* you can!" Ben said it in a way that everyone else knew they could do it, too.

"Now, Newby," Ben said, looking at the little dog who had worked his way into the middle of the circle. "Tell us if we're going to be *awesome!*" Everyone laughed when Newby barked once, really loud, but then they got quiet again. Ever so gently, Ben squeezed Carrie's hand, and she squeezed J.J.'s, and he squeezed Kelly's, and she squeezed Yonah's, and she squeezed Matt's, and he squeezed Liza's, and she squeezed Storm's, and he squeezed Mrs. Blake's. When the squeeze got back to Ben, it was time to go.

12

CURTAIN CALL

Carrie swayed back and forth on the front porch, taking each item out of the shoe box and looking at it again. The morning edition of *Mountain Views* lay open tent-style over one arm of the rocker. The play had made the front page yet again. Her mother sat down beside her and began to rock, too. "The newspaper had some nice things to say about you," she said, trying to balance a Styrofoam cup of coffee on one arm of the chair. Carrie nodded.

"The article forgot to mention that Liza Barrett accidentally stepped on her own long petticoat and danced right out of it in the middle of her biggest scene," her mother said, but not unkindly. "I couldn't believe that she was standing there and never missed a line. She kept on singing and dancing as if no one would even notice."

"Ben said the show had to go on, no matter what," Carrie said. She stood up and tossed Yonah's yo-yo over her hand. It got stuck at the bottom of the string.

"And I still can't even believe that Newby just took it in his teeth and dragged it offstage, as if the whole thing had been planned all along."

"Storm told him to," Carrie said, untangling the knot. "Newby always does what Storm says." She tried to yo-yo again.

"Storm was really great. His mother and Uncle Will were so proud they couldn't stop clapping."

"Storm was awesome!" Carrie agreed.

"You *all* were," said D.D., sitting down in the rocker on her other side. Carrie had been thrilled to see D.D. enter the Apple Barn the night before—in plenty of time.

"I've never seen anybody so happy as old Will Sellers when he won that dilapidated truck at the intermission," Mrs. O'Connor said. "What a strange door prize—giving the oldest vehicle in town to the oldest person at the play! Wonder who thought of that?"

Carrie turned her back and kept tossing the yo-yo so her parents wouldn't see her smile. "Santa Sellers finally got his sleigh back," she whispered to no one in particular.

"I don't know," said her father, "but I'm just glad I didn't win it. I don't think that truck would ever make it to New York City."

"I don't think it wants to leave here anyway," Carrie said as she tossed the yo-yo out again.

"Here's something else for your shoe box." D.D. handed Carrie a large brown envelope. "It's from your mother. I forgot to give it to you last night."

Carrie unfastened the metal prongs that held the flap and looked inside. "What is it, Mom?" she asked.

"The book I told you about. The first one I ever wrote. I think you're old enough to appreciate it now."

It was written on white construction paper and tied together with thin blue ribbon. On the cover were three drawings. In one, a tall boy and a long-bodied dog had climbed halfway up a mountain. Another showed two children holding up a fish. The third was of a rabbit.

Beneath the pictures, in a child's crooked writing, was the title "A Book for My Brother." Underneath the title, in smaller letters, it said, "by Kate McCarrity." Carrie opened the book to the first page and began to read.

I remember playing paper, scissors, and stone out back on our porch. Only you never hit my hand hard when you won.

I remember when we skipped school and went down to the drugstore for cherry sodas. And you said if I ever told, you'd break my big toe off. Only I didn't have to tell because we got caught anyway.

I remember the time Wally Barrett called me four eyes when I had to get glasses, and you told him if he ever called me that again, he'd only have four teeth.

I remember how you hated to help with the dishes when it was your turn so you traded me ten dish washings for one ride on your shoulders all the way up the hill and down again.

I remember when you got straight A's and you made me promise not to tell your friends so they wouldn't call you bookworm like they called LeRoy Mills.

I remember how I bit your hand when we were saying grace on Thanksgiving, only you couldn't holler until Dad said A-Men.

I remember how hard you laughed when you found my doll in the refrigerator where I'd put it so it wouldn't get so hot in the summer.

I remember how your jersey smelled when you came home from a baseball game. And how you'd pitch to me real easy and call me Slugger, though I never hit a thing.

I remember how much you liked the birthday

presents I gave you—the picture of the mountain with you and Dory climbing up it . . . the fish I brought to you on your fishing pole because I couldn't get the hook out by myself. How Mom took a picture of us with that fish before you took it back to the pond and let it swim again. How you helped me frame that picture with Popsicle sticks.

I remember when you helped me catch a rabbit in a box out back and we named it Ears. Then we let it go, too.

I remember when Thomas Boone gave you a home-run ball he had caught at a Cardinals' game when he visited St. Louis, and you let me take it to show-and-tell.

I remember when you named my rag dolls Lucy and Ethel and made up jokes for them to tell each other before I went to bed at night.

I remember how you never went anywhere without Dory, and how you used to sneak him scraps from your plate when you thought no one was looking.

I remember when you pretended to have a sore throat so Louis the Loser Sanders could take your big role in the school play and he wouldn't have to feel like a loser anymore.

I remember how you taught me to climb to the top of the jungle gym on the playground.

"Just look at where your foot is going, but re-member where it's been."

Carrie closed the pages gently and hugged the book to her. "But, Mom," she said at last, "you put all those things in the Michael Madigan books."

Her mother nodded silently, fingering the side of the coffee cup.

"So Michael Madigan was really . . ." Carrie didn't have to finish her sentence. Her mother nodded again.

"And Ben Sanders . . . does his first name happen to be Louis? As in, Louis the Loser Sanders?"

"The *L* does stand for Louis, if I remember correctly."

They sat there, the three of them, rocking silently.

"Love lives on in curious ways, doesn't it?" D.D. said at last. Then he got up and moved to stand behind Carrie's chair.

"If you've got the afternoon off, Madame Molar," he said, "I think there's bound to be a mountain around here somewhere just begging to be climbed. Can you be ready in five minutes?"

And he softly scrambled the hair on the top of her head.